EX LIBRIS

THIS BOOK BELONGS TO:

WARNING! DO NOT USE YOUR REAL NAME!

"THE OLD GAMES WITHIN GAMES, SMOKE AND MIRRORS, CIRCLES WITHIN CIRCLES. YOU CAN GET A LITTLE LOST SOMETIMES."
—JONNA MENDEZ

A NOTE ON THE ART

Since you are the kind of keen-eyed reader who can spot a note like this amidst all the boring letters and numbers on the copyright page, you will probably also notice something interesting about the pictures in this book: Oftentimes the text will describe something as one color, and the illustrations will show that thing in a completely different color. That's because we printed this book using only three colors: black, red, and a yellowish color we call "Freddie Orange." So no matter what color things were in real life (because, of course, this book is about my real life), in this book they are either black, red, or Freddie Orange. (Or white—that's where we didn't use any ink at all.) Anyway, this is just to say: We meant to do that! We like the way it looks.
—M.B.

To Mike Lowery
— M.B.

Dedicated to my buddy Mac B. Look, Mac! You got your name in the book!
— M.L.

Text copyright © 2021 by Mac Barnett • Illustrations copyright © 2021 by Mike Lowery
All rights reserved. Published by Orchard Books, an imprint of Scholastic Inc., *Publishers since 1920.* ORCHARD BOOKS and design are registered trademarks of Watts Publishing Group, Ltd., used under license. SCHOLASTIC and associated logos are trademarks and/or registered trademarks of Scholastic Inc. • Game Boy is a registered trademark of Nintendo Co. Ltd. • The publisher does not have any control over and does not assume any responsibility for author or third-party websites or their content. • No part of this publication may be reproduced, stored in a retrieval system, or transmitted in any form or by any means, electronic, mechanical, photocopying, recording, or otherwise, without written permission of the publisher. For information regarding permission, write to Scholastic Inc., Attention: Permissions Department, 557 Broadway, New York, NY 10012. • This book is a work of fiction. Names, characters, places, and incidents are either the product of the author's imagination or are used fictitiously, and any resemblance to actual persons, living or dead, business establishments, events, or locales is entirely coincidental.
Library of Congress Cataloging-in-Publication Data available
ISBN 978-1-338-74245-9
10 9 8 7 6 5 4 3 2 1   21 22 23 24 25
Printed in China   62 • First edition, May 2021
The text type was set in Twentieth Century.
The display type was hand lettered by Mike Lowery.
Book design by Doan Buu

MAC B.

KID SPY

MAC SAVES THE WORLD

WINK

By **Mac Barnett**

Illustrated by **Mike Lowery**

Orchard Books
New York
An Imprint of Scholastic Inc.

ME AS A

~~KID~~

SPY!

FROM THE DESK OF

MAC BARNETT

MY NAME IS MAC BARNETT.
I AM AN AUTHOR. BUT
BEFORE I WAS AN
AUTHOR, I WAS A KID.
AND WHEN I WAS A
KID, I WAS A (SPY).

AN AUTHOR'S JOB IS TO
MAKE UP STORIES. BUT
THE STORY YOU ARE
ABOUT TO READ IS TRUE.

THIS ACTUALLY HAPPENED
TO ME.

This is my dad's house.

It is on the top of a hill in a town called Oakland, California. That's a real place. You can look it up.

When I was a kid, every other weekend I went to my dad's house.

This was one of those weekends.

I was downstairs playing video games.

My dad and my stepmother were upstairs, watching TV in their bedroom, with the door closed.

My heart was pounding, and not just because I was eating some Cinnamon Toast Crunch I'd poured into a cup, even though it was against the rules to have food downstairs at my dad's house.

Mainly my heart was pounding because I had a secret mission.

I am a little nervous to tell you about this secret mission.

If you've read other books in this series, you'll know I usually put *lots* of secret spy stuff in them. One of them is even called *Top Secret Smackdown*.

Look! It says "top secret" right there on the cover!

Normally when you put spy secrets in a book, you get thrown in spy jail.

But the stories in these books took place a long time ago, all the way back in the year 1989.

After a long time passes, spy secrets get "declassified." That means you're allowed to put them in books, and nobody throws you in spy jail.

Except the secret mission I had at my dad's house is not a spy secret.

It is a family secret.

Family secrets never really get declassified.

When you put family secrets in books, your family gets mad at you, which is worse than spy jail.

I should know. I went to spy jail once! And my family has been mad at me. More than once!

This is why many authors write fiction. When you write fiction, you can put your family secrets in books, but just say everything is made up. When your family calls you all mad, you can say, "This book isn't about us! My name is Mac, and the main character's name is Steve!"

But the main character of this book is named Mac. The main character of this book is me.

And I will tell you my mission, even though it was a family secret.

WINK

My mission was to sneak a bunch of tiny bars of soap from my dad's house to my mom's house.

I can explain.

Sort of.

See, my dad was a dermatologist.

And my stepmother was also a dermatologist.

That means that they were doctors who treated people's skin.

And *that* meant that they got lots of soap samples sent to their house, for free.

They had a closet full of tiny bars of soap.

And so whenever I went over to my dad's, my mom asked me to load up my backpack with soap and smuggle it back to our house.

That way she didn't have to buy soap.

You might be wondering: Mac Barnett, why didn't your mom just ask your dad for some of his extra soap?

Sometimes I used to wonder that too, when I was a kid.

(I still do.)

Families can be complicated.

Anyway, I had a mission.

I peeked upstairs to make sure my dad and stepmother were still in their room, watching TV, with the door closed.

They were.

I got to a place in my video game, SPY MASTER, where there were no KGB agents trying to kill me, and put the controller down without pausing. That way, the

SPY MASTER theme song would keep playing, and if my stepmother poked her head out from their bedroom, it would sound normal downstairs.

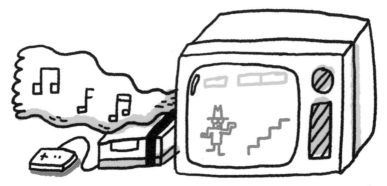

Plus the SPY MASTER theme song was really exciting!

I hid my cup of cereal behind a sofa cushion, in case my stepmother came downstairs.

I ducked behind the couch.

I avoided the creaky floorboards.

I tiptoed toward the closet with all the soap in it.

I slowly turned the doorknob and pulled the door open, careful not to leave any fingerprints behind.

Not because they dusted their soap closet for fingerprints.

Their whole house was painted white, and whenever I got smudges on the walls, my stepmother asked my dad to have a Talk with me.

That was one of the rules at my dad's house: no smudges.

(There were lots of rules at my dad's house.)

Inside the closet, I gingerly pulled a beaded chain to turn on the light.

They kept their soap stashed on a high shelf, so I stood on a box to reach it.

Just as I was looking at all the different kinds of soap, the phone rang.

Good! Nobody ever called me at my dad's house. They would be distracted while I loaded up my back-pack with all this soap!

From upstairs, my dad yelled, "Mac, phone!"

I froze.

Then I unfroze.

I hopped off the box, turned off the light, opened the door, and swiftly shut it behind me. My dad was coming down the hallway!

What are you doing?" my dad asked.

"Just going on a walk," I said. "A walk down the hall."

"With your backpack?" he asked.

"Yep," I said.

He stared at me.

"OK," he said.

He held out the phone.

I grabbed it fast.

My dad kept looking at the door behind me.

He frowned.

I turned around to see what was bothering him.

FINGER PRINT
SMUDGES !

My dad sighed.

"Sorry," I said.

He sighed again.

I put the phone up to my ear.

It was the Queen of England.

3

COMPUTER

"Hello?" I said.

"Hullo," said the Queen of England. "May I speak to Mac?"

"Speaking," I said.

"Mac," said the Queen of England, "what are you up to?"

I thought for a second.

"I can't say," I said.

"You can't say!" said the Queen of England. "When I asked you, I was just being polite, but now I actually want to know!"

"It's a secret," I said.

"Now you must tell me," said the Queen of England. "I love secrets!"

"It's a *family* secret," I said.

"Well, you can tell me in person," said the Queen of England. "I need you to come to England right away. A car is waiting outside your father's house to take you to the airport. I'm afraid I need a rather urgent favor."

"What kind of favor?" I asked.

"Well, if you must know, I have a mission for you."

"What kind of mission?" I asked.

"A secret mission," said the Queen of England. "And I will tell you my secret when you tell me yours. Good-bye."

4

QUEEN
SACRIFICE

"Why doesn't your mother just ask your father for some of his soap?" asked the Queen of England.

She was sitting on her throne, in her throne room, in England.

"I don't know," I said.

I was kneeling in front of her throne, in her throne room, in England.

"Well, I'm sorry to take you away from your secret mission in order to send you on a secret mission."

"It's OK," I said. "You're saving me from having to have a Talk with my dad."

"About the soap?" asked the Queen.

"No," I said. "I smudged the walls."

"You what the what?"

"No smudging the walls," I said. "It's one of the rules of the remodel."

"The what of the what?"

"My stepmother remodeled the house, and there are all these rules about walls and carpeting and towels and stuff."

The Queen raised her eyebrows and said, "I see."

"It's hard to remember, because at my mom's house, there's a whole different set of rules," I said.

"Such as?"

"Such as . . ." I thought. "Such as don't wake her up early on the weekends and no playing with matches."

The Queen nodded. "Sensible rules. Mac, may I ask you a question?"

"Of course!" I said.

"Why are you kneeling?" asked the Queen of England.

"I don't know," I said.

I was a kid from California, and I still didn't really understand when you were supposed to kneel while talking to the Queen. So, just to be safe, I tended to kneel.

The Queen sighed. "What *do* you know?"

I didn't answer, because I figured it was a rhetorical question.

"That was not a rhetorical question," said the Queen. "I am really asking. For instance, do you know about computers?"

I stood up and smiled.

"Yeah!" I said.

"Wonderful!" said the Queen of England. "Can you help me save my game?"

"Are you playing a video game?"

"Certainly not!" The Queen of England sniffed. "I am playing computer chess."

She rang a silver bell.

"Alister! Humphrey! Bring in my computer!"

Two men in suits wheeled in a computer on a fancy table.

There was a green-and-black chessboard on the monitor, with the pieces scattered all around.

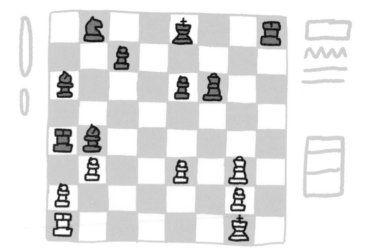

"Do you have a floppy disk?" I asked.

Floppy disks were big square pieces of plastic with a magnetic circle in the middle that could store information. They were floppy. (Good name.)

It was really fun to wave them in the air. They would wobble and make a funny bendy sound. But then your computer teacher would yell, "You'll ruin the disk!"

"Of course I have a floppy disk," said the Queen. "Bartholomew!"

Another man in a suit brought in a floppy disk on a silver tray.

"First, I will make my move." She peered at the computer monitor. "You see, I am in the middle of a match against my son, the Prince of Wales—"

I giggled.

"That is Wales the country, without an 'h,'" said the Queen of England. "He is not a marine mammal."

"I know," I said.

"Then stop giggling," said the Queen.

I stopped giggling.

"Before we were able to finish our game, the Prince of Wales—you're giggling again—had to leave for a polo match. And so after I make my move, I would like you to save my game to that disk, which we will fly via helicopter to West Sussex, whereupon my son will be able to load it on a computer and make his move! Oh, the marvels of modern technology!"

The Queen used a mouse to click on a pawn.

The cursor hovered over a square.

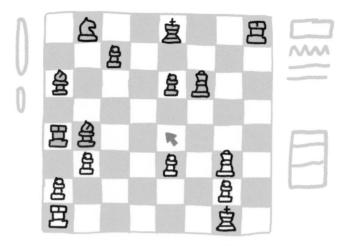

"Ooh," I said. "I don't think you want to do that."

The Queen squinted at me. "And why not?"

"Well, see, in chess you have to think a few moves ahead. If you move your pawn there, he can move his bishop there, and you'll be in check, so then you'll have to move your queen here, and then he'll take your queen, and you'll be in checkmate. You'll be all out of options. You'll lose."

"Very interesting," said the Queen.

Then she ignored my advice and moved her pawn anyway.

"But—" I said.

"Mac," said the Queen. "I'm trying to lose. I wish to let my son win."

"Oh!" I said. "That's really nice!"

"That way," said the Queen, "he will become over-confident and, foolishly believing he is smarter than me, my son will play sloppily, allowing me to beat him handily for the next six matches at least!"

"Hmmm . . . ," I said.

"A Queen sacrifice! Losing to win!" She tapped the side of her crown with her index finger. "You see, Mac. You are thinking a few *moves* ahead. But I am thinking in *matches*. Now save my game."

"OK." I put the floppy disk in the computer and typed some commands on the keyboard.

There was a whir, and some clicking, and a few seconds later, the game was saved.

"Done!" I said.

I took out the floppy disk and waved it in the air so it wobbled.

The Queen of England frowned at me.

"Does that ruin the disk?" she asked.

"Um," I said.

Alister, Humphrey, and Bartholomew also frowned at me.

I stopped waving the disk and handed it to her. "Here you go."

"Well done." The Queen of England nodded primly. "You have passed the test. Your secret mission will re-quire these amazing skills. For it involves the high-tech world of supercomputing!"

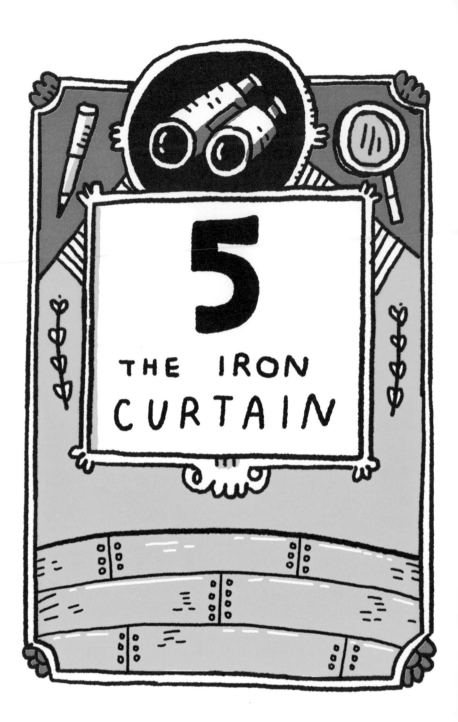

5

THE IRON CURTAIN

Allister, Humphrey, and Bartholomew were dismissed.

"Mac," said the Queen. "Your mission is very dangerous. It will take you across the Iron Curtain."

"OK," I said.

"Do you know what the Iron Curtain is?"

"No," I said.

The Queen of England sighed.

"As you well know," said the Queen, "for decades we have been in constant struggle with our great foe, the Soviet Union."

I did well know! I knew because my archenemy was a spy for the KGB, which was the spy agency of the Soviet Union, which is a country that does not exist anymore.

The KGB Man sowed chaos and destruction wherever he went. Plus one time he had stolen my blue jeans and never gave them back.

"This struggle is called the Cold War," said the Queen. "It is a war fought with stories and spies. And it is a war in which many countries have picked sides."

"Like kickball," I said.

"Excuse me?" said the Queen.

"At school, every day at recess all the kids play kickball," I said. "Derek Lafoy and Michaelanne Petrella are the two most popular kids in my class, and they're always team captains, and then the rest of us play on their teams."

"Whose team are you on?"

"I don't play kickball. I'm not really an athlete."

"I am aware," said the Queen of England.

"You are?" I said.

"Indeed," said the Queen of England. "I have seen your President's Fitness Test results."

I went pale.

Every year when I was a kid, we spent a week of PE taking the President's Fitness Test. If you did a bunch of push-ups, sit-ups, and pull-ups, you passed, and you got a certificate signed by the president of the United States of America.

(That's true. You can look it up.)

I never passed the President's Fitness Test. Derek Lafoy would always come by and wave his certificate in my face while singing "The Star-Spangled Banner."

"Whatever, Derek," I would say, "that's not his real signature."

Derek insisted it was, but I figured the president of the United States had better things to do than keep track of how many pull-ups I could do.

"Wait," I asked the Queen of England. "How do you know my President's Fitness Test results?"

"The president of the United States told me."

"He did?"

"Yes. We are friends. In the Cold War, America and Great Britain are on the same side. You see, Mac, there is a line running down the middle of Europe. Countries west of that line are on our team. Countries east of that line are on the Soviets' team. And that line that divides our continent in twain is called . . ." The Queen leaned forward. ". . . the Iron Curtain."

I pictured a huge metal wall running across the middle of Europe.

"Of course," said the Queen, "the Iron Curtain is not an actual wall."

I stopped picturing a huge metal wall.

"These countries are divided by laws, and loyalties, and ideas," said the Queen. "The Iron Curtain is simply a name."

"Good name," I said.

"It is," said the Queen of England. "People will tell you a man named Winston Churchill came up with that name, but he did not. In life you will find that whenever somebody says something clever, Winston Churchill usually gets the credit and very rarely deserves it."

"So it's an imaginary wall," I said.

"Indeed." The Queen tapped her temple, right below her crown. "The Iron Curtain exists only in our minds. But that does not make it any less real."

"OK . . . ," I said.

The Queen's voice grew hushed. "But there is a place where the Iron Curtain *is* an actual wall."

I pictured a huge metal wall again.

"But it is not made of metal," said the Queen.

I decided to stop picturing things until the Queen told me more about this wall.

"Where is it?" I asked. "And what's it made of?"

"I shall tell you a story," said the Queen. "In 1961—"

"Oh boy," I said.

6

THE
WALL

"*In 1961*," said the Queen of England, "early one Monday morning in Berlin, a man named Hagen Koch went on a walk."

"Is this an interesting story?" I asked.

The Queen regarded me coolly. "It is a very interesting story," she said. "Because in 1961, Berlin was a very interesting place. For even though Berlin was one city, it existed in two different countries.

"The western part of the city belonged to West Germany, and the eastern part of the city belonged to East Germany.

"Let me know if you need me to slow down," said the Queen of England. "I am aware that many Americans are allergic to geography."

"I'm not allergic to geography," I said. "I'm allergic to cod!"

"Cod?" said the Queen.

"It's a type of fish," I said.

"I know what cod is. I did not know one could be allergic to it."

"It's actually the third most common non-shellfish fish to be allergic to," I said.

The Queen stared at me.

"Anyway, I like geography," I said.

"Good," said the Queen. "Now, speaking of geography, where were we?"

"Berlin."

"Yes!" said the Queen. "One city in two different countries. In 1961, you could walk from East Germany to West Germany, and back again, by simply crossing the street."

"Neat!" I said.

"Indubitably," said the Queen of England. "But every day, hundreds of East Germans walked across the street and never crossed back. They escaped to West Berlin and stayed in the west. This made the head of East Germany furious, and the head of the Soviet Union furious too. They were on the same team.

"And so the East Germans and the Soviets got to-gether and devised a way to stop people from leaving. They rolled out barbed wire, right in the middle of the streets. People panicked! They crawled under the wire, and tore their clothes and cut their skin! West Berliners held out blankets for East Berliners who jumped out of windows into West Berlin. But then East German sol-diers bricked those windows right up."

"That's terrible!" I said.

"Indeed," said the Queen. "And it gets even worse. That day was Stacheldrahtsonntag, which is German for 'Barbed Wire Sunday.' The next day, a Monday, a man named Hagen Koch went on a walk."

Now I was interested.

"He had a can of paint," said the Queen, "and a paintbrush. And as he walked across the city, he paint-ed a line on the ground.

"And where that man had painted a line, the East Germans built a permanent wall.

"The wall has separated neighbors, friends, and families. For thirty-eight years, it has cut the city in two. The Berlin Wall is twelve feet high and ninety-six miles long. It is made of reinforced concrete. It is patrolled by East German soldiers, guarded by fierce dogs, and loaded with traps and trip wires. And you are going to cross it."

7

FLOPPY DISK

"Why?" I said.

"The Soviet Union and East Germany are allies. That means the two countries are very close friends. And just like close friends, they often communicate in a secret code, a special language only they two understand."

"OK," I said.

"Who is your best friend, Mac?"

I thought for a second. "Probably you," I said.

"Ah," said the Queen. "I see. Well . . ."

"And we *do* have a secret way of talking only we two understand! Like when you say 'indeed,' it means you're really happy with me! And when you interrupt me and say my name, it seems like you're being really stern and cold, but usually you're cutting me off because you're uncomfortable showing your feel—"

"Mac," said the Queen.

I smiled.

"Enough!" said the Queen of England. "Stop smiling. The secret messages from the Soviet Union to East Germany are unbreakable. Unless . . ."

"Unless?"

The Queen of England rummaged in her handbag and pulled out a photograph.

"Mac, take a look at this computer."

"It's huge!" I said.

"Yes," said the Queen. "And you know what they say about computers: the bigger the better."

(People no longer say that.)

"This computer," said the Queen of England, "is called the Robotron 2000."

"Good name," I said.

"Indeed. The Robotron 2000 is located on the top floor of the tallest building in Berlin: the Television Tower."

"Good name!" I said.

"Mac," said the Queen of England, "I need you to sneak into the Television Tower and find the Robotron 2000!"

"Wow," I said.

"The Robotron is an East German computer programmed with powerful Russian cryptography software. It is the only machine capable of decoding certain very important messages that pass be-tween the Soviets and the East Germans. And you, Mac, are going to steal it."

I stared at the photograph.

"It looks really heavy," I said. "I don't think I can carry it."

The Queen frowned. "Not the computer, Mac! You're going to steal the software."

She held up the floppy disk. "You're going to find the supercomputer and save the encryption program to one of these disks, whose name I find ridiculous and refuse to say. Then we'll be able to listen in on all the secret conversations the Soviet Union is having with East Germany!"

"High-tech!" I said.

"Indeed," said the Queen of England, waving the floppy disk so it wobbled.

"I think that actually might ruin it," I said.

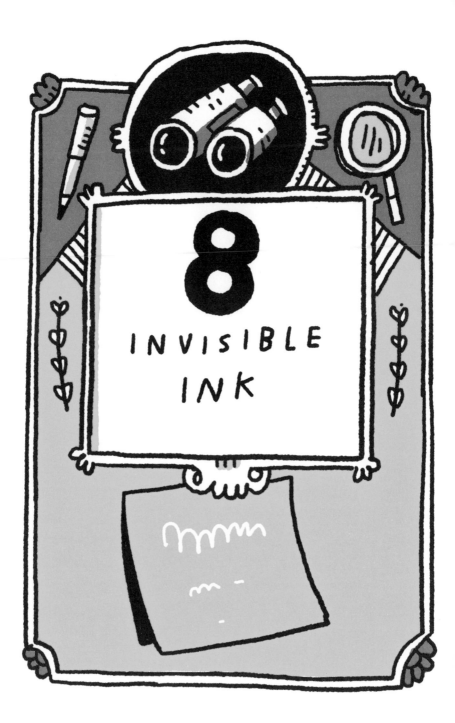

"You will, of course, need some spy gear," said the Queen of England.

"Cool!" I said.

She handed me a pen.

"Ooh." I held it up to the light. "Does it explode?"

"Of course not!" said the Queen. "And if you really thought it might, you should not be holding it like that."

I peered at it. "Is there a tiny camera inside?"

The Queen shook her head. "Sounds expensive."

This was disappointing. "So it just writes?"

"No," said the Queen. "There's no ink in it."

This was too much.

"Well, what does it do, then?!" I asked.

The Queen smiled and produced a lemon, which she tossed to me.

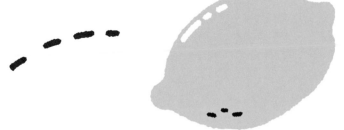

"An ordinary pen and an ordinary piece of fruit," said the Queen. "But dip the nib of the pen in lemon juice and you will have your very own homemade invisible ink!"

She passed me a piece of paper.

The paper felt very fancy.

She clapped her hands together. "Try it!" she cried.

"OK," I said. I thought for a while.

Then I peeled the lemon, cupped my hand, and squeezed some juice into it.

As soon as I'd finished writing out my secret message, the Queen held out her hand.

"Pass it here! Pass it here!"

I did.

"Now we wait for it to dry." The Queen covered her eyes. "I'm not peeking!"

We waited.

Finally, the Queen held the message above a candle stuck in a fancy gold candelabra near her throne.

"When exposed to flame," said the Queen, "the message will reveal itself!"

As if by magic, my writing appeared in big brown letters.

"How exciting!"

The Queen read my message.

"That's it?" The Queen frowned.

"I couldn't think of anything," I said.

"Hmmm," said the Queen.

"I was on the spot!"

"Well, it certainly lacks zing," said the Queen. "And your handwriting is not much improved."

"I'm working on it!" I said.

"In any case," said the Queen, "if I need to communicate anything very important to you, I will do so using invisible ink!"

"OK," I said. "Do I need a candle, then?"

"Dear no!" said the Queen. "You are a child! Just hold it up to a light bulb. Like your mother says, no playing with matches! Or was that your father?"

"My mom," I said.

"It's hard to keep track," said the Queen.

"Yeah," I said. "One family, two rule books."

"You should feel very much at home in Berlin," said the Queen. "Be careful. Take Freddie with you. Good luck."

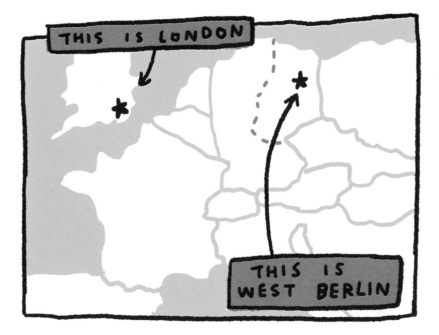

Freddie was a dog.

He belonged to the Queen of England, but I think he liked me better.

I liked having him along on my missions, but he wasn't a trained spy dog or anything.

Mostly he just licked stuff.

For instance, he spent a lot of the train trip to West Berlin licking my face.

I didn't like it when Freddie licked my face, but I also kind of did like it.

It was nighttime when we arrived in West Berlin.

I had instructions to find an old theater in the middle of the city, where I would pick up my secret identity.

Since I had been on so many spy missions, I had been "burned." That means other spies knew I was a spy.

So the East Germans wouldn't let me cross into their country. Unless I was in disguise.

I walked down crowded streets lit by flashing lights.

For a while, the sidewalk ran right along the Berlin Wall.

The wall rose high above my head. It was covered in murals and writing. I could have reached out and touched it.

But I didn't.

I was afraid to.

I turned a corner and walked a few blocks until I arrived at the right address.

The building was huge. It looked like an ancient temple made out of wedding cake, the kind of place you might go to hear an opera.

But the music drifting out of the building was definitely not opera.

It was loud and thudding.

Inside, it was even louder. And thudding-er.

Disco balls and chandeliers hung from the ceiling, scattering neon light all over the room.

Smoke machines on the floor belched thick fog.

On the stage, a band was playing.

They were wearing safety-orange jumpsuits that glowed under the stage lights.

But instead of musical instruments, they were hunched over computers.

It sounded like video game music, but much, much louder!

The dance floor was packed with people doing wild moves.

I tried not to look amazed so I could fit in.

But it was hard not to look amazed.
Everybody's outfits were so cool!
A bunch of people were wearing leather jackets.

One person looked like she
was wearing clothes made out
of chessboards.

Another guy was wearing
a suit that was way too big
for him.

I wished I had my best pair of blue jeans, which were perfectly faded.

But like I said, they'd been stolen by the KGB Man. I looked at my shorts, forlorn.

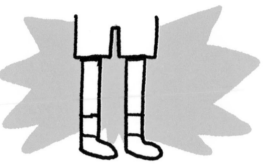

But there was no time to feel bad for myself! I was on a mission.

I danced over to a man who was standing by the stage with his arms crossed. He had lots of tattoos.

"Schöner Hund," said the man.

I had no idea what that meant.

I looked at my hand.

DANKE

HALLO

TSCHÜSS

HUND

WO IST DIE TOILETTE?

3RD STALL FROM LEFT.

PFERD

"Wo ist die Toilette?" I asked.

That means "Where is the bathroom?"

"Nach unten."

I smiled and nodded.

I had no idea what that meant.

"What?" I said.

"Downstairs," said the man.

"Thank you!" I said. I checked my hand. "Danke!"

The man didn't say anything.

Everything in the bathroom downstairs was covered with graffiti. The walls, the sink, even the paper towel dispenser. Bare pipes ran across the ceiling.

"Don't lick anything," I told Freddie.

I could still hear the music down here, but it sounded like I was underwater.

I checked my hand again and entered the third stall from the left.

Then I locked the door behind me, took the lid off the toilet tank, and reached inside.

Now, wait! Before you think I'm really gross, re- member: A toilet tank is full of *clean* water. So it wasn't gross.

Still, I felt kind of gross.

But a toilet tank is an excellent place to hide secret stuff. (Because nobody checks there, because it seems gross.)

I pulled out a plastic bag.

The bag was opaque, so I tore it open to see what was inside.

There was a safety-orange jumpsuit.

A wig.

Sunglasses.

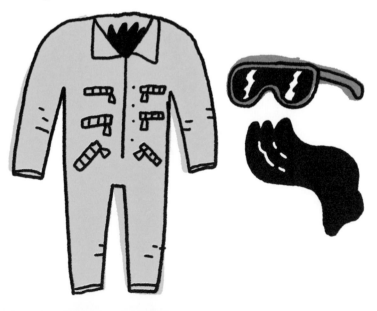

And a fake passport with a picture of a guy who looked like this:

I put on my disguise and looked in the mirror.

"To the max!" I said, which is something I'd heard cool people say on TV.

(People no longer say that.)

10

WEST BERLIN

WEST BERLIN

EAST BERLIN

I felt something in one of the pockets of my jump-suit.

(The jumpsuit had so many pockets!)

I unzipped it (the pockets had zippers!) and couldn't believe what I found.

A Game Boy cartridge!

I already owned this game.

"Aw man." I put my hand on my hip.

And I felt something in another pocket of my jump-suit!

(I told you it had a lot of pockets!)

It was a letter from the Queen of England.

HULLO!
CONGRATULATIONS ON YOUR
TRANSFORMATION! THESE IDENTITY PAPERS
WILL ALLOW YOU TO CROSS INTO EAST
BERLIN. IF I KNOW YOU (AND I
KNOW YOU VERY WELL!) YOU ARE
PROBABLY DISAPPOINTED BY this
GAMEBOY GAME! WELL, IT'S NOT
ACTUALLY A COPY OF ELEVATOR
ACTION. WAIT TILL YOU FIND OUT
WHAT IT REALLY DOES!

HERE IS THE PLAN:

The rest of the letter was blank.
Invisible ink!

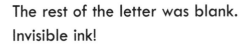

I rushed to the sink and held the Queen's letter up to the light bulb.

Letters appeared!

(Unfortunately, we could not print these books using lemon juice, so even if you hold the letter up to a lamp, you won't be able to know what the Queen said. Sorry!)

"So *that's* what this video game does," I said to myself in the mirror.

"Ha ha, that's such a funny joke!" I said as I kept reading the letter.

"Wow, this is probably the best letter I've ever read!" I said. "To the max!"

This is Checkpoint Charlie.

Checkpoint Charlie was a gap in the Berlin Wall where you could pass from one side of the city to the other.

Ever since Berlin was divided in two, the west side of Checkpoint Charlie was guarded by American soldiers.

Instead of saying the letter "C," American soldiers sometimes say "Charlie"—that way it's easier to understand on a walkie-talkie.

So Checkpoint Charlie was just another way of saying Checkpoint C.

(Checkpoint Charlie is a much better name.)

You could only pass through the checkpoint if you had the right papers.

I had the right papers.

Although those papers were fake.

But hopefully nobody would notice that.

It was before dawn, and Checkpoint Charlie was quiet.

Thick mist hung in the air.

Tall streetlamps cut through the fog.

I approached a white sign with big black letters.

YOU ARE LEAVING
THE AMERICAN SECTOR
ВЫ ВЫЕЗЖАЕТЕ ИЗ
АМЕРИКАНСКОГО СЕКТОРА
VOUS SORTEZ
DU SECTEUR AMÉRICAIN
SIE VERLASSEN DEN AMERIKANISCHEN SEKTOR

The sign made me gulp.

A soldier popped out of a little metal shack.

I handed him my papers.

He took a quick look at them and waved me through.

I walked along a metal fence.

A watchtower rose up in front of me.

I could make out the silhouettes of two soldiers up there.

I could tell they were soldiers from their big caps.

And although I couldn't see their eyes, I knew they were watching me.

I hugged Freddie close.

We were passing sandbags and fences.

I was crossing from one country to another.

I was straddling the Iron Curtain.

At one moment, maybe that very moment, my body was in two worlds at the same time.

I was afloat, I thought, a ghost on a map drifting—

"Your documents."

A stern East German soldier interrupted my thoughts.

He was standing in front of a striped barrier.
"Right, sorry," I said.
I handed them over.
He looked at them for a long time, frowning.

"Smile," I thought to myself. "Look friendly."
I smiled friendlily.

The soldier looked up and noticed my smile.
He kept frowning.

"What do you do, Mr. Gibson?"
"You can call me Billy," I said.

"I have to call you Mr. Gibson, Mr. Gibson."

"OK," I said.

We stood in the mist, looking at each other.

"Oh! Right! You asked me a question," I said. "What do I do?"

"Yes."

"What do you mean?"

"Your business, Mr. Gibson."

"Oh," I said. "I'm a musician. I'm in a band."

"And what is the name of this band?"

I was not expecting so many questions.

"Oh . . . ," I said. "We're called the Cyber Punx."

"The Cyber Punks?"

"Punx. With an 'x.'"

"And this dog, he is also in the band?"

"Um," I said. "Yes."

The soldier's eyes widened. "I was joking," he said.

"I wasn't," I said.

When you are lying, you often have the urge to tell more lies to make your first lie seem more convincing. This is almost always a bad idea.

"We just played a show," I said. "It was such a good show!"

"You just played a show?" said the guard.

"Yeah!" I said.

"And where are your instruments?"

I smiled harder, to buy myself some time to think.

The soldier's frown deepened.

I took my Game Boy out of my backpack.

"This is my instrument."

"A Game Boy," he said.

"Yeah," I said. "It's the future of music. Check it out."

I turned on my Game Boy.

The SPY MASTER theme started playing.

I turned the volume all the way up, but the music was swallowed by the night.

"And the dog?" said the soldier.

"He barks," I said. "When he feels like it. It's art."

The frowning soldier held my documents in the air.

"You are telling me that you are in a band, with a dog, calling yourselves the Cyber Punks—"

"With an 'x,'" I said.

"With an 'x,' and your music is just video game sounds and a barking dog?"

"Yes," I said.

He stared at me.

I gulped.

"To the max!" said the soldier.

He smiled.

I was already smiling.

He lifted the barrier.

I turned down a dark alley, took off my wig, and tossed it in a trash can.

I had crossed the Iron Curtain.

14

THE TOY
STORE

My first stop was a toy store tucked on a quiet street.

I loved visiting toy stores.

(I still do.)

When I walked up, the shopkeeper was turning the sign on the door from GESCHLOSSEN to GEÖFNETT.

She smiled at me.

A bell rang when I pushed the door open.

The shop was filled with toys I'd never seen before.

Board games.

Play sets.

Computer chess.

They all looked so fun!

But I wasn't here for fun.

I had a job to do.

Behind the counter, a bunch of hats hung on hooks.

I just pointed to a shiny black helmet.

She handed it to me.

I unzipped another one of my pockets and passed
her some money.

She gave me my change.

"Danke," I said.

She smiled and watched me as I left the store.

I looked over my shoulder one last time when I was
on the street.

She was still watching me.

This is the Urania World Clock.

It's in a plaza below the Television Tower.

Urania is the Greek muse of astronomy.

On the Urania World Clock, beneath a model of the solar system, a dial with the numbers one through twenty-four slowly spins through the twenty-four time zones of the world.

You can find out what time it is anywhere in the world by walking around the clock.

It was 7:00 p.m. in Berlin, where I was.

It was 6:00 p.m. in London, where the Queen of England was probably sitting down for a big feast.

It was 10:00 a.m. in California, where I lived.

It was time to move.

16

THE
TELEVISION
TOWER

This is the Television Tower.

It's a big tower with a television broadcast antenna at the top.

(Good name.)

In 1989, the tower was almost 1,200 feet tall, a sleek column topped by a huge ball with a sharp spike sticking out the top.

I stared up at the Television Tower.

Somewhere up there, behind a locked door, the Robotron 2000 clicked and whirred.

Down below, in a plaza, my brain clicked and whirred too.

Through a set of big glass doors, I watched people milling about in the lobby.

On the back wall, there were two sets of elevator doors.

Every few seconds, the doors on the left would slide open.

People would exit the elevator.

Other people would enter the elevator.

The doors would close, and the elevator would go up.

You know, normal elevator stuff.

But the elevator doors on the right never opened.

Nobody got on or off.

And this elevator was guarded by a uniformed man.

This was not normal elevator stuff.

This was *secret* elevator stuff.

It was time to don my next disguise.

I put on the helmet I'd just bought at the toy store.

"Wish us luck, Freddie," I said.

He wasn't listening to me, because he was distracted by some pigeons.

I pushed through the doors of the Television Tower. We were in!

I strode across the lobby with great confidence, walking straight for the secret elevator.

I pretended like the guard wasn't even there.

If I didn't acknowledge him, he'd think I knew what I was doing and wouldn't stop me.

"Halt!" said the guard.

He was speaking German, but I knew what he was saying, because we also have that word in English.

I halted.

I tapped my helmet and said, "Feuerwehrmann."

I was speaking German, but only because I had spent a chunk of the morning memorizing that word.

It meant "firefighter."

And the hat on my head was an East German fire-fighter's helmet!

Firefighters get to go pretty much anywhere, and nobody asks them any questions.

The guard asked, "Und was ist mit dem Hund?"

Now I had no idea what he was saying.

But he was pointing at Freddie.

Luckily I had memorized another German word that morning.

"Feuerwehrhund," I said.

That meant "fire dog"!

"Ich habe keine Ahnung was das ist," said the guard.

I still had no idea what he was saying, and I was all out of German words, so I gave him a thumbs-up.

Then I pressed the call button.

The doors opened.

I stepped in the elevator.

I gave the guard another thumbs-up.

The doors closed.

I pushed the button for the top floor.

The elevator zoomed up.

17

ELEVATOR
ACTION

Classical music was playing.

We were rising so fast my tummy fluttered.

Then the elevator lurched to a stop.

A little bell rang.

The doors opened up to a revolving restaurant.

There were white tablecloths on every table.
Huge windows looked out on the city.
People ate lobster and slurped soup.
The maître d' looked surprised to see me.
I pointed to my helmet.
"Feuerwehrmann," I said.
I pointed to Freddie.
"Feuerwehrhund," I said.
I gave a thumbs-up.

The elevator doors closed.

I sprang into action!

I used both hands to press every button in the elevator at the exact same time.

The buttons all lit up, and a panel on the wall flipped open.

Behind the panel, there was a screen, with an outline of a hand.

If you used a special light bulb to read the Queen's secret message on page 58, you know just what that was.

It was a fingerprint scanner!

Of course, I did not have the right fingerprints.

But if you read the Queen's secret message, you'll know exactly what I did next. In fact, I probably don't even need to tell you!

18
HACKER STUFF

But I will tell you.

I whipped off my backpack and took out my Game
Boy.

I put in the game from the Queen of England.

I unplugged a wire from the fingerprint scanner, jacked it into my Game Boy, and flipped the switch on.

Normally a game's start-up screen said something like "PRESS START TO BEGIN."

But now my screen was different:

I pressed start.

A lion's head appeared on my screen.

Every time the lion opened its mouth, numbers came out of it.

The wire sizzled.

The Game Boy screen went black.

The handprint glowed red.

A computer voice said, "Zugriff gewährt."
Everything was quiet.

"I don't know what that means!" I said. "What does that mean? Is it good or bad?"

A trapdoor opened in the ceiling of the elevator.

"It was good!" I cried.

I picked up Freddie.

He looked happy.

But he usually looked happy.

Still, I could feel his tail wagging against my chest.

I pushed him up through the trapdoor, then climbed up after him, into the darkness.

19

COMPUTERRAUM

I was in an elevator shaft, surrounded by steel cables.

The classical music trickled out through the trapdoor and bounced off the walls.

In the dim light, I could make out a door before me. Yellow letters on the door read:

"Finally!" I said. "Something I can read."

Freddie stared up at me.

"It means 'Computer Room,'" I said.

Freddie kept staring up at me.

"Or, on second thought, it could also mean 'Computer RAM,'" I said.

Freddie stared.

"See, RAM is a type of computer memory," I explained to Freddie.

He just stared back.

"Probably 'Computer Room' though," I said. "I don't know why a door would say 'RAM.'"

I opened the door and stepped through, into the Computer Room.

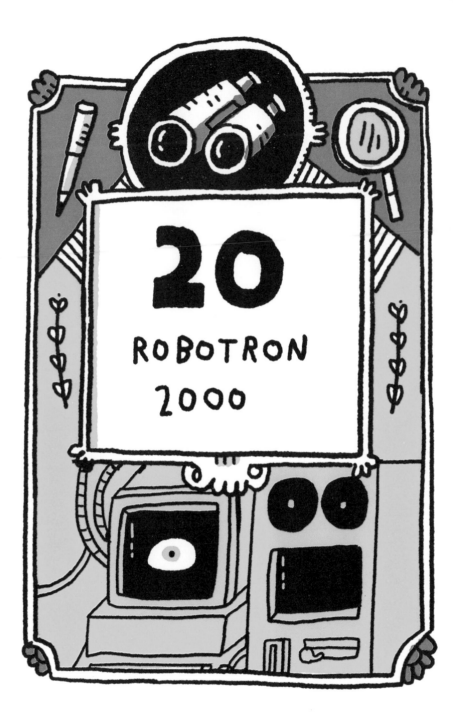

The only light in the room came from a glowing green monitor on a desk: a screen that displayed a huge green eye.

The eye stared at me.

I stared back.

That was it: the Robotron 2000.

Wires ran everywhere, out from the Robotron, covering the floor like poisonous snakes. I picked up Freddie to make sure he didn't step on any of them, or lick any of them, which would be even worse.

I approached the computer slowly.

The green eye blinked.

Was it scared?

Was it angry?

Did it want me to leave?

Could the Robotron see me?

Was it alive?

Had the East Germans and the Soviets collaborated to create an artificial intelligence? An all-seeing, all-thinking, all-feeling computer that would mean certain victory over the West?

"Freddie, don't!" I cried.

But Freddie didn't listen.

He never listened.

Freddie wriggled out of my arms, put his front paws on the desk, and licked the Robotron, right on the eyeball.

His right paw landed on the space bar.

The eye disappeared.

"Oh," I said.

It was just a screen saver.

Screen savers are little animations old computers
would play so their monitors wouldn't burn out.

(Good name.)

"Nice work, Freddie!" I said as I picked him up from the desk, because he was still licking the Robotron.

Now the screen was black except for a little blinking green rectangle in the upper-left corner.

This rectangle was the cursor.

It was waiting for me to write.

"Let's do this," I said.

I put on some special computer gloves.

They were black, and the fingertips were cut off.

This way my knuckles would stay nice and warm, but my fingers could type fast.

I took out the floppy disk and slid it into the computer drive.

I ran my hands through my hair.

I put on my sunglasses, then took them off, because it was too hard to see.

I cracked my knuckles.

The cursor blinked.

I typed.

```
C:\>copy secretcodes.exe A:\>_
```

I pressed return.

I pumped my arm.

"Cybertastic!" I said, because I thought it would be a cool thing to say in that moment.

(It wasn't.)

A little red light lit up on the Robotron.

The computer made a bunch of terrible clunking and scraping sounds!

It's OK: That's just what it used to sound like when you saved a file to a floppy disk.

A status bar showed up on the computer screen.

The Robotron clunked, and it scraped, and a couple of times it even screeched, as it copied the secret Soviet encryption software onto the floppy disk.

I drummed my fingers on the desk and waited for it to finish saving.

"Yes!" I cried. "Halfway there!"

I wondered if watching the screen was making it feel like it was taking longer, so I looked up at the ceiling and counted to a hundred, then looked back.

"Aw man," I said.

"Here we go!" I said. "Just one bar left!"
My fingers hovered next to the disk drive.

"Come on!" I said. "It's going backward!"

26

CYBERTASTIC

Look, it took a really long time, but eventually the file finished saving.

I pulled out the disk.

"Cybertastic!" I said again, to see if it felt cooler the second time I said it, because maybe the reason it didn't feel cool the first time was just that it was a new word that had never been said before.

(It's always good to test out new slang terms alone a few times before you say them in front of anyone, just so you don't embarrass yourself.)

"Wow, what a dumb word," somebody said behind me.

I whipped around.

There, blocking the door, stood the KGB Man.

He was wearing a KGB officer's hat.

A KGB officer's coat.

And my American blue jeans.

"How did you know I'd be here?" I asked.

"I got a phone call," said the KGB Man. "An anonymous tip! A woman told me to look out for a kid in a firefighter's helmet!"

"Aw man," I said.

"And now," said the KGB Man, taking a step toward me, "you will please hand over the floppy disk. Did I say that right? Floppy disk?"

"Yeah," I said.

"What a silly name," said the KGB Man.

He took another step. My back was pressed against the desk.

The room was small, too small to squeeze past him. I looked around, panicked.

There was a door to my left! I hadn't noticed it before!

"The disk!" The KGB Man made a grasping motion. "I demand it!"

"Fine," I said. I held out the disk.

But just as he was about to grab it, I shouted, "Psych!"

I whipped back the disk and ran for the door!

"Psych your mind!" I shouted over my shoulder.

As I got closer, I saw the door had a word painted on it in very serious yellow letters:

ACHTUNG!

I could figure out what that meant: "ACTION!"
And this was definitely a time for action!
I pushed through the door!
And then I almost fell off the side of
the Television Tower.

I was on a narrow catwalk more than one thousand feet in the air.

The wind was whipping.

The lights of the city twinkled below me.
I gripped Freddie tight.
Behind me, the KGB Man was rushing for the door.
I sidled along the catwalk, keeping my back
against the cold metal of the tower's sphere.

The KGB Man stuck his head out the door.
He looked down, then back at me.
His eyes were wild with fear and fury.

"You fool!" he shouted. "Don't you know what 'ACHTUNG' means?"

"I thought it meant 'ACTION,'" I said, sidling.

"It means 'DANGER,'" said the KGB Man.

"That makes sense!" I said.

The KGB Man stepped through the door and prowled along the catwalk.

He was quicker than I was, but I had a head start.

The catwalk wound upward round and round the big metal ball.

The KGB Man was closing the distance between us, but I was afraid to sidle faster. I didn't want to slip and then fall off the tower, and then . . .

It was better not to think about it.

The catwalk ended abruptly at a landing on the top of the big metal ball.

A huge TV antenna rose up beside me—the tip-top of the tower.

My stomach hurt and my eyes watered.

"This must be how an ant feels, standing atop a marble, stuck on top of a pencil," I said.

"What did you say?" shouted the KGB Man.

I didn't know he'd gotten close enough to hear me.

"I said," I said, "this must be how an ant feels, standing atop a marble, stuck on top of a pencil!"

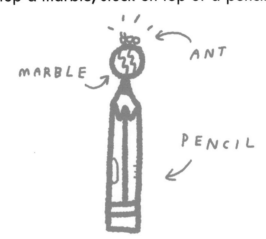

The KGB Man paused and frowned.

"What in the world are you talking about?"

I shrugged.

"I was just talking to myself," I said.

We faced off atop the sphere like two angry ants, fighting over a marble.

The KGB Man inched closer.

I knew I'd lose this fight.

I put Freddie in my backpack to keep him safe and placed the floppy disk between my teeth.

Then I climbed up the TV antenna.

29

TIP-TOP

I arrived at the tip-top of the tower.

My feet were 1,198 feet above the ground.

That meant, even though I was the shortest boy in my class, my head was over 1,200 feet above the ground! Neat!

The wind was really whipping now.

There were dark clouds in the sky.

I hoped that didn't mean lightning.

If there was any lightning, it was definitely going to strike me, on top of this tower. I would get shocked, and then I'd fall off the tower, and then . . .

It was better not to think about that either.

I looked down.

The KGB Man was below me, on the ladder, looking up.

"There's nowhere left to go!" he shouted. "Give up! Hand me the disk!"

"Never!" I said.

I held the floppy disk above my head.

It was probably about 1,202 feet above the ground.

The floppy disk wobbled in the wind, making a bendy sound.

"Now I see why they call it a floppy disk!" the KGB Man said. "Good name!"

"Yeah!" I said.

I was worried all this flopping was going to ruin the disk.

Which brought up a big question: If you couldn't wobble a floppy disk without ruining it, *was* it actually a good name?

There was no time to answer this question though.

I had an archenemy to outwit, a disk to smuggle, a mission to accomplish.

I looked at the city spread out below me.

To the east, a bunch of bright lights.

To the west, more, even brighter lights.

And below me, the Berlin Wall, a dark scar across the middle of the city, a void interrupted only by the roving beams of searchlights.

If only I had a portable hang glider in my backpack, I could soar through the sky, over the wall, and land in West Berlin, with the disk.

But I did not have a portable hang glider.

I didn't even know if a portable hang glider existed.

Lightning struck!

Not actually.

What I mean is, I had an idea.

30

A BOLD PLAN

This was my idea:

I could throw the floppy disk over the wall, into West Berlin!

But:

Could I throw the floppy disk over the wall, into West Berlin?

The wall was a few blocks away.

And I definitely could not throw a ball a few blocks.

I could not throw a ball from second base to home plate, which is why Derek Lafoy and Michaelanne Petrella didn't pick me for their kickball teams.

But that was on the *ground*.

I was over 1,200 feet in the air!

So didn't that mean I could throw something really, really far?

And a floppy disk was different from a ball.
It was more like a Frisbee.
Or even a hang glider.
A tiny, portable hang glider.
"A hang glider for ants!" I said.
"What?" said the KGB Man.
"Watch this!" I said. With a flick of my wrist, I
launched the floppy disk toward West Berlin.

The disk caught a gust of wind and sailed in the
direction of the wall.

But after a few feet it stopped sailing. It began
plummeting.

The floppy disk dropped over 1,200 feet, straight down, and landed in the plaza with what I could only imagine was a sickening slap.

"Aw man," I said.

The KGB Man and I looked at each other for a moment, perfectly still except for our hair flapping in the wind.

Then he grinned and began to clamber down the ladder.

It was a race to the bottom!

And the KGB Man had a head start!

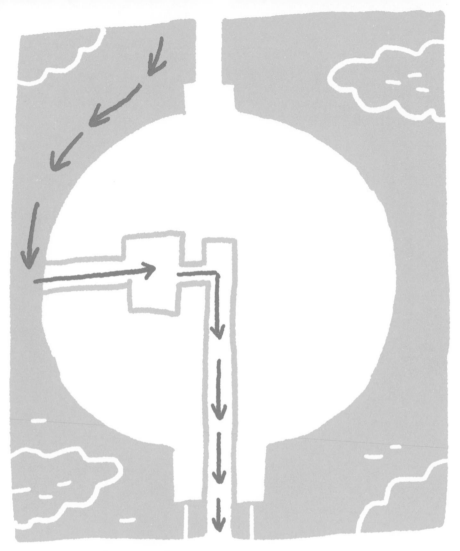

Down the tower!

Around the ball!

Into the Computer Room!

I chased after the KGB Man.

He hopped down the trapdoor, into the elevator car, but I managed to squeak in before he slammed it shut.

We faced off in the cramped car.

He reached forward with both arms.

I thought he was trying to put me in a bear hug, so I ducked.

But instead he pushed a button on the elevator's controls.

The bell dinged.

The doors opened.

He shoved me into the fancy restaurant.

The maître d' was even more surprised to see me this time.

"Table for one!" the KGB Man shouted. "Ha ha ha ha ha ha . . ."

As the doors closed, he laughed and laughed. I could hear his laughter getting farther away.

The elevator was going down!

I gave the maître d' another thumbs-up and made for the stairs.

There are 986 steps in the Television Tower.

I took them two at a time, stopping on each floor to press the call button outside the elevator.

That way, the KGB Man would have to stop on every floor.

Now it was my turn to laugh!

I couldn't laugh that hard though, because I was out of breath.

By the time I reached the ground floor, I had a cramp in my side.

But I sprinted through the lobby, out into the plaza.

In the streetlamps' electric light, I searched desperately for the floppy disk.

I peered down at the ground, rushing to and fro.

Several Germans asked me questions, but I couldn't understand what they were saying.

The KGB Man burst forth from the tower.

He started combing the other side of the plaza.

I had to find that floppy disk!

Wait—over there!

A small crowd had gathered by a bench.

I rushed over.

Several people were listening to an old lady.

She was pointing up at the sky with one hand.

In the other hand, she was holding the disk!

She wobbled it. It was making the bendy sound.

She laughed, and so did the people around her.

"Stop!" I said. "You'll ruin the disk! Even though it's called a floppy disk, you're not really supposed to wobble it!"

"Wat?" she said.

She continued to wobble the disk.

By now the KGB Man had noticed the commotion.

He was on his way over.

I pointed to the disk.

"That's mine!" I said. "Mine!"

"Wat?" said the old lady.

The crowd was beginning to grumble.

I pointed to the disk one more time and shouted, "Achtung! Achtung!"

The lady yelped and dropped the disk.

The crowd backed away.

I snatched it from the ground and took off running.

I sprinted through the streets willy-nilly, making lefts and rights on a whim. I had no idea where I was, so it didn't matter where I was going.

The city was busy. People were out on the sidewalks.

Cars were on the roads.

In front of an alley, a woman grabbed me by the shoulders and, grinning wildly, shouted, "Die Mauer ist offen!"

"I don't speak German!" I said, wriggling free.

"Die Mauer ist offen!" she yelled after me.

I ran away.

As I passed a bright yellow phone booth on a corner, it began to ring.

33

EXTRACTION

RIINNG

"Hello?" I said.

"Hullo! May I speak to Mac?"

"Speaking," I said.

"Mac! This is the Queen of England," said the Queen of England. "How's it going?"

"OK," I said. "I have the disk! But the KGB Man is chasing me."

"Oh dear," said the Queen.

"I need to get out of East Berlin fast."

"Oh dear dear dear," said the Queen of England. The line got quiet.

But the streets were loud.

People were shouting.

Horns were honking.

"What is going on over there?" the Queen asked. "I can scarcely think!"

"I think there's a parade," I said.

"At this hour?"

"Or party?"

"Typical Berliners," said the Queen. "What are they going on about?"

I listened. "They're shouting, 'Die Mauer ist offen!'"

"And what does that mean?" asked the Queen.

"I don't know," I said. "I don't speak German."

"Nor I," said the Queen. "Well, we can't send you back through Checkpoint Charlie. They'll be looking for you. I suppose you'll have to sneak out."

"Sneak out?"

"Yes," said the Queen of England. "People have been sneaking across the Berlin Wall from the beginning. Tunnels, mostly, although the East Germans have discovered most of those. And it would take too long to dig a new one, probably. Are you particularly quick with a shovel?"

"No," I said.

"No," said the Queen, "I shouldn't think so. I wonder if the old spot is still good. Well, let's hope so! I'll give you directions. Write this down."

I took out a pen and looked at the palm of my left hand.

There wasn't much room. I had to write small.

34

THE
CLIMB

The Queen's directions took me to a quiet neighbor-hood.

I went down an alley, climbed over a fence, and followed some train tracks.

I ducked under a hedge, into a garden.

There, in an old potting shed, was a ladder, just as the Queen said there would be.

I carried the ladder with me, and some pruning shears too, out of the garden and down a very narrow street, where the buildings stood close together, then suddenly stopped.

There was a chain-link fence topped with sharp wire, and then a huge empty strip—no trees, no build-ings, nothing—and beyond that rose the wall.

A dog barked in the night.

Freddie barked back.

I crept up to the fence and, quietly as I could, used the shears to cut a hole in the links.

A bright beam of light from a nearby guard tower moved back and forth along the empty strip.

I waited till it passed right in front of me.

Then, through the dark, I ran.

I made it to the wall.

There were no murals, no paintings on this side.

Just cold, dark concrete looming tall in the night.

I leaned my ladder against it and began to climb.

But when I got to the top of the ladder, the wall was still too tall.

Or I was too short.

I couldn't reach the top of the wall.

I stood on my tiptoes.

I reached with my right arm, and then with my left,

in case one of my arms was longer than the other.

But it was no use.

"OK, Freddie, hold on tight," I said.

I stuck the disk between my teeth, raised both arms above me, and jumped as high as I could.

I was able to grasp the top!

Two black leather boots appeared on the wall above me.

They were tucked into a pair of perfectly faded blue jeans.

"Need a hand?" said the KGB Man.

35
DANGLING

"Aww mnf," I replied, because I was biting down on the disk.

"Did you really think you could escape me?" said the KGB Man. "Ha! Wow! If you did, that's really dumb!"

"Inf nunf fnnf," I said.

My sneakers kicked against the concrete as I tried to scramble up the wall.

"I am afraid," said the KGB Man, "that you are all out of moves. You are stuck."

I struggled to lift myself onto the wall.

My biceps burned.

The KGB Man smirked.

"It's no use." He reached into the pocket of his coat and withdrew an official-looking document that he waved in front of my face.

My vision was blurry, but I could make out a blue eagle.

"A spy in the White House has provided me with a copy of your President's Fitness Test results."

He pretended to peruse the piece of paper.

"Can this be right? Zero pull-ups?"

It was right.

When I was a kid, I couldn't do any pull-ups.

(I still can't.)

During the President's Fitness Test, I would just hang from the pull-up bar until the PE coach blew his whistle and I could drop back down to the ground.

"Hmfhg ninf msk," I said.

"Here, let me help you," said the KGB Man.

He bent down and plucked the disk out from between my teeth.

"Aw man," I said.

The KGB Man shook his head. "As the expression goes, you were so, so close to making it, but they ran out of cigars."

"That's not an expression," I said.

"Whatever!" said the KGB Man. "Expressions are hard in English! Look, just to show you I have soft feelings, I'll pull you up!"

The KGB Man extended his right hand.

Using the last of my strength, I raised a hand up toward his.

"Psych!" he cried. "Psych *your* mind!"

And he hopped down off the wall, doing a neat

little roll as he hit the ground. He began running across the strip, back toward East Berlin.

He waved the disk wildly above his head.

"You shouldn't do that!" I shouted. "You'll ruin the disk!"

"I don't care!" he said. "You're the one who wanted it! Ha ha ha ha ha ha!"

"Oh yeah," I said.

He climbed over the chain-link fence and disappeared into the night.

"I won!" he cried, and was gone.

Exhausted, I dropped back down onto the ladder.

I was still trapped behind the Iron Curtain.

How was I going to escape?

Would I have to live in East Berlin for the rest of my life?

Or at least until I got tall enough to use this ladder?

If so, I was going to have to start learning German.

I didn't even know how to say hello!

"Guten tag," said someone up above me.

"I don't know what that means," I said.

"It means, 'hello.'"

I looked up.

There was an old man standing on the wall.

"You speak English?" the man said.

"Yeah," I said.

"No German?"

"Not really. A little bit. Feuerwehrmann. Feuerwehrhund, achtung. Oh, and"—I looked at my palm—"Wo ist die Toilette?"

"Some very useful things to know!" said the old man. "And also some less useful things."

"Yeah," I said. "Oh, and I can say 'Die Mauer ist offen!' but I have no idea what that means."

The man laughed.

Suddenly, I remembered to be surprised.

There was an old man standing on the wall!

"What are you doing?" I said. "You're not supposed to be up there!"

The old man laughed.

"And you're not supposed to be down there! What a night!"

"Yeah, but—"

He reached out his hand. "Here, come up! The dog first."

Even though he was old, he was strong. He lifted us onto the wall.

"Thanks," I said. "But—"

"Die Mauer ist offen!" The man laughed again. "That means 'The wall is open!' I saw it on TV. They said, 'The East Germans have opened the checkpoints! People are crossing to West Berlin! From the west and

the east, people are climbing the wall and the soldiers are doing nothing to stop them!'"

He pointed over his shoulder. "I live right there. In that house! In the west! I saw them put up this wall. Twenty-eight years ago! Outside my window they built this . . . thing! I hate it! And when I saw the people climbing, the people on TV, I said, I am going to climb that wall!"

"Why is this happening?" I asked.

The man said, "I have no idea!"

We both laughed.

37

THE
FALL

I'll tell you a story.

On November 9, 1989, a man named Günter Schabowski went on TV.

He worked for East Germany.

That night, he was supposed to announce that, sometime in the future, East Germany was planning to make it easier, temporarily, to cross over to West Germany.

But he was tired that night.

And the lights on the TV cameras were bright and hot.

He was sweaty.

And when someone asked him when East Germans would be allowed to cross into West Germany, he looked down at his papers.

And because it was bright, and he was sweaty, and it had been a long day, he said, "As far as I know, um, now, immediately, without delay."

But he was wrong.

That wasn't what it said on the papers.

It was a mistake.

But his mistake made it onto the news.

And when people heard, they flooded the streets.

Thousands gathered at the checkpoints.

And the soldiers at the checkpoints didn't know what to do.

They decided to open the wall.

Berliners climbed up on the wall.

People who hadn't seen one another for thirty years hugged and kissed.

People who'd never met one another in their whole lives hugged and kissed.

They danced.

They sang songs.

They brought hammers and started chipping away at the wall.

That is how it happens.

One moment a wall is patrolled by guards and dogs.

The next moment people are dancing on it.

Just because a guy named Günter read a piece of paper wrong.

It's pretty wild.

But it's true.

You can look it up.

38
IN FROM THE COLD

Of course, I didn't find out that whole story until later, when I got back home, to California.

I gave my mom a hug. And a bunch of tiny soaps.

She was really happy to see me!

I took my backpack up to my room.

Normally when I completed a mission, there was a gift from the Queen.

But this time there wasn't anything. Probably because my mission had failed.

But I hadn't been back for more than five minutes when the phone rang.

I didn't answer it.

(I was kind of dreading talking to her.)

The phone stopped ringing.

Then it started ringing again.

I sighed.

Then I answered it.

"Hello?" I said.

"Hullo!" said the Queen of England. "May I speak to Mac?"

"Speaking," I said.

"Mac, are you avoiding my calls?"

"Well," I said, "yes."

"But we have to have our debrief after the mission! It's tradition!"

"OK," I said.

"Mac," said the Queen, "have you figured out who told the KGB Man you were in the Television Tower?"

"Yes," I said. "The woman at the toy store."

"No!" The Queen giggled. "It was me!"

"What?" I said. "You ruined the whole mission!"

"Wrong!" said the Queen. "The mission was a success!"

"But it failed!"

"Yes! All according to my plan!"

"Your plan?" I said.

"Yes!" said the Queen of England.

"But I thought you needed the disk to read Soviet codes!"

"No!" said the Queen. "That's just what I told you! You see, we have a top secret computer even *bigger* than the Robotron 2000. The Evesham 3000! Isn't that a wonderful name?"

"Yeah," I said.

"Anyway," said the Queen, "the Evesham 3000 can decode anything. Of course, if the Soviets knew that we could read their codes, they'd just build an *even bigger* computer. A Robotron . . ."

"4000," I said.

"Yes!" said the Queen. "Precisely. And so I sent you into East Berlin to try to convince the Soviets that we needed to steal their technology! Isn't that clever? It was a mission designed to fail!" I could hear the clinking of her finger tapping her crown. "A Queen sacrifice!"

"You could have told me," I said.

"Of course I could not have," said the Queen. "I needed you to really *mean* it."

"Hmm," I said.

"Don't be cross!" said the Queen. "You did brilliantly! By failing at your mission, you may have saved the world."

"I think I'd better go."

I hung up on the Queen.

I sat at my desk.

I felt a bit glum.

There was a piece of paper on my desk that didn't belong there.

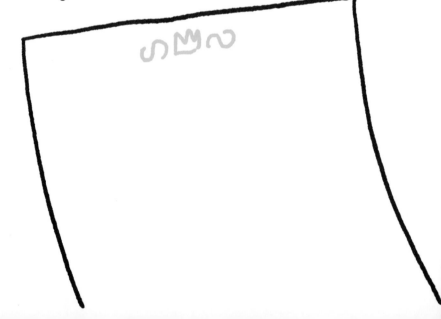

I flipped on my desk lamp.

Under the bulb, a secret message appeared.

Dear MAC,
I am WRiTing you this letteR
Because I imagine you are going
to hang up on me when I tell
you the true nature of your mission.
I know you VERY WELL! That is why
I selected you for this _VERY_
important Task!

To thank you foR youR
SeRvice, I have gotten you
yet another gift, even though
you NeveR seem particularly
excited about my gifts.
ANyway, youR PResent is in
the top drawer of youR DResseR.

I stopped reading the letter and ran to my dresser.

There was a box in the top drawer, tied with a
shiny bow.

It was a pair of blue jeans!

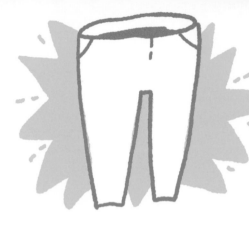

I held them up in the light.
They were perfectly faded.
I kept reading the letter.

I KNOW you've Been wanting some new Jeans ever since yours got stolen, because you NEVER stop talking about them. AND So, all's well that ends well! HOW wonderful!
Still, I own no Jeans and am perfectly satisfied.

My Majesty,
The Queen of England

PS. you mentioned that I was your Best Friend. Like many women my age, I No longer organize my Friends in ORDER of "Best," "Second-Best," ETC. It's all a bit Ridiculous. HOWEVER I am very fond of you, and you're my Best friend too.

PPS. Please eat this letter NOW. Even though it's written in invisible ink, I can't have it falling into the wRong Hands.

As soon as I'd finished reading, the phone rang.

Again.

It was the Queen of England.

Again.

"Hello?" I said.

"Hullo!" said the Queen of England. "May I speak to Mac?"

"Speaking," I said. "Do I really have to eat this?"

"Of course!" said the Queen. "You certainly can't burn it. That would be dangerous!"

"Aw man," I said.

I tore off a corner.

"Before you begin chewing," said the Queen, "I need to ask you a question, and I would not have you speak with your mouth full. Mac, will you do me a favor?"

I smiled.

I said, "OK."

Mac Barnett is a *New York Times* bestselling author of children's books and a former ████████████. His books have received awards such as the Caldecott Honor, the E. B. White Read Aloud Award, and the Boston Globe-Horn Book Award. His secret agent work has received awards such as the Medal of ████████████, the Cross of ████████████, and the Royal Order of ████████████ ████████████ the Third. His favorite color is ████████. His favorite food is ████████. He lives in Oakland, California. (That's true. You can look it up.)

Mike Lowery used to get in trouble for doodling in his books, and now he's doing it for a living. His drawings have been in dozens of books for kids and adults, and on everything from greeting cards to food trucks. Mike is the author and illustrator of *Random Illustrated Facts*, and the books *Everything Awesome About Dinosaurs and Other Prehistoric Beasts* and *Everything Awesome About Sharks and Other Underwater Creatures,* with more Everything Awesome series titles to come. Mike lives in Atlanta, Georgia, with a little German lady and two genius kids.